WILLA'S ADVENTURE

Julia Barnes

CHAPTER 1

Happy Birthday!

Once upon a time, there was a 7-year-old girl named Willa. Well, she was almost 7 years old. Her birthday was on Saturday. She was SUPER excited, and will have a party! The theme is princesses. When I say the word "princesses" you may think of Belle, Ariel, Tiana, etc. But the princesses I'm talking about are the Water princesses. There are 8 Water princesses:

1. Lindsay the lake princess
2. Rebecca the river princess
3. Pia the pool princess
4. Octavia the ocean princess
5. Cecilia the current princess
6. Gwen the gulf princess
7. Hazel the hose princess
8. Bethany the bubble princess

Each girl has a necklace that has magic. Lindsay has lake magic; Rebecca has river magic; Pia has pool magic, etc.

Willa's favorite princess was Bethany the bubble princess. She wanted to be like her, all the bubbles and stuff. Willa did not know it, but Willa was secretly sisters with the Water princesses! Plus, Willa did not know that she was a Water princess - of waterfalls! Each gift from her friends was swim stuff because she liked to swim. She had a gift from her mom and dad: Willa will live with the Water princesses! Wow.

At the birthday party, everyone who Willa invited was there. Because she was a Water princess her birthday was in summer, and Willa loved to swim! Her mom would cook up a barbecue, her dad would set up the pool, and her friends would splash. Willa would swim very gracefully, and Willa liked that a lot. On every birthday that she had she loved to swim.

After the birthday party, Willa's mom and dad led Willa to a big gray sphere. Willa's dad explained, "This is a rainbow pod. It is a special transportation system that will take us to where we are moving."

"MOVING? On my birthday?" sobbed Willa. A little tear went down her cheek.

"No worries, Willa. We are moving the house with us in the rainbow pod!" said Willa's dad. Willa smiled after this.
"Where are we going?" asked Willa.

"A surprise!" said Willa's dad. Willa was very happy. She could not wait! After Willa's mom packed the house and everything, Willa was filled with questions. She asked her dad: "Are we moving because of my birthday? Or do you guys want to camp? Or are we going to live with someone else?"
Willa's dad laughed as he said, "You will see."

When they got to the other side of the rainbow, Willa's dad said, "Here we are." When Willa poked her head out of the window, she saw a lake, a river, a pool, an ocean, a current, a gulf, a huge hose, bubbles, and a waterfall. There was also a big well next to the bubbles.

Willa's eyes shimmered. She had never seen anything so beautiful! There was one girl in each of those things. Then Willa's mom put the house behind the waterfall. Willa stared at all the girls. "Lindsay, Rebecca, Pia, Octavia, Cecilia, Gwen, Hazel, and Bethany. What?" Willa whispered.

"Hi, Willa," said Bethany. "I am your sister!"

"That's crazy! WAIT! If you are magical, how come my parents aren't magical?" asked Willa. Bethany replied: "Well, it happens. And you are a Water Princess, too!"

"What? But…" said Willa.

"Yep." Bethany interrupted. "Please behold our new Water Princess: Willa, the princess of waterfalls!" Hazel placed a necklace on

Willa's neck, and a crown on Willa's head! Willa was so happy that she leaped through the waterfall. She was happy that she moved, plus she loved hanging out with her sisters. It was the best surprise ever!!!!!!!!

CHAPTER 2

Time to Learn

Two days later, Willa was sitting on her bed, wide awake. She put on a dress her dad made for her and her favorite crown of all. She met Lindsay at her house, then the 9 sisters ate pancakes- Willa's favorite! Willa knew she would have gone to a different school this year, but did not miss her old one. Willa was proper; she knew her manners and used them, she was a real rule follower! Now she went to a proper school, where everyone was a rule follower. Rebbecca, Octavia, Gwen, and Bethany were in the same class as Willa.

All five girls rode in a carriage pulled by pegasi to the open house (that was their "car"). On a normal day of school, they would ride in a flying school bus. Today the girls will get to know what their classroom looks like, who their teacher is, and where their desks are. The treehouses were the classrooms. The five girls acquired their supplies for school! So that's good.

On the first day of school, all nine princesses met at the bus stop. The bus was just like Willa's old bus, but it could fly! When the bus was almost there, Willa could not believe her eyes. There was a huge, rainbow cloud with a school on it and treehouses! The bus parked on the cloud. When they got off, Willa went with her sisters to the school. The school was amazing and colored gold. "Princess Elementary." read Willa.

Rebecca, Octavia, Gwen, Bethany, and Willa walked to their classroom; right where they found it before at the open house. "Good morning, class!" said Willa's teacher, Mrs. Mikaela. "For now, you will color a picture. If you look at your desk, you will see a coloring page. All papers on your desk in the morning will be called morning work." The princesses did the coloring page. It was a butterfly.

At 9:15 a.m, "RING, RING, RING," rang the bell for the morning. "Princesses," called Mrs.Mikaela. "Morning work is over. If you are not done, then you can save it to work at home. Now please come to the carpet." All the princesses walked to the carpet. Willa was so happy. All the children at her old school *ran* to the carpet! Instead of shapes on the carpet, there were crowns. The princesses were listening to the teacher. The children at Willa's old school *talked*, not listened! "Today, we will write a story. It can be anything you like. Let's watch a short video to help." Willa could not believe her ears. She loved writing! She already had an outstanding idea.

When the video was over, Mrs.Mikaela said, "Now, please go write your story." The princesses were already at their desks after the video was over. Willa wrote: *Once upon a time, there were two girls. The two girls were named Sweet and Sour. Both of them adored cooking and wanted to open a restaurant. Their dad named Kevin, and their mom named Holly, and their three sisters, Salty, Bitter, and Umami, wanted to help make the restaurant. The restaurant was finished after quite some time. Now Sweet and Sour wanted to find magical cookbooks. They searched near a couple of huge hills. Finally, Bitter dug somewhere not far away from the hill and saw five cookbooks that are labeled: Sweet, Sour, Salty, Bitter, and Umami.*

"RING." rang the recess bell. "Now that the recess bell has rung, please line up. Alyssa, go first. Bethany, go second. Chya, third. Faelynn, fourth. Gwen, fifth. Kairi, sixth. Octavia, seventh. Rebbeca, eighth. Vesta, ninth. Willa, tenth. Yeilia, eleventh." All the princesses walked down the hall which was marked with street signs! When they got to Playground Avenue, the princesses ran and played. They were so energetic!

After recess, Willa sat near Rebbecca, Octavia, Gwen, and Bethany at lunch. Gwen and Rebbecca needed to buy lunch. So Octavia and Bethany were already at the table. "Hi, Willa," said Octavia.

"What have you got for lunch?" said Bethany.

"Hmmm, let me see," said Willa, as she opened her lunch box. It had a crown on it. "I have a sandwich, mac and cheese, yogurt, and pretzels."

"I have chicken, fries, broccoli, and bananas," said Octavia.

"I have an orange, a butterfly-shaped salad, cheese, and a slice of cake," said Bethany.

Soon after, Gwen and Rebecca were out of the hall where princesses buy lunch. "We both got the special: Spaghetti and meatballs!" said Gwen. Willa saw Lindsay, Pia, Cecilia, and Hazel at the table that was behind Rebbecca, Octavia, Gwen, Bethany, and Willa.

When lunch was over, the lunch teacher, Ms. Lacy said, "5,4,3,2,1." Immediately the princesses silenced. 5,4,3,2,1 means it's a countdown and if any princess talks after the countdown is finished, then the others will wait. "Very good." Ms.Lacy happily said. "Lunchtime is over. Please clean up quietly." Ms.Lacy commanded, and the princesses did exactly what Ms. Lacy said. *I like this school!* Willa thought. Willa put her sandwich, mac and cheese, yogurt, and pretzels in her lunch box. The princesses who bought their lunches put the trays in the compost.

Now, Willa, Kari, and Octavia were headed to their math class. "Alright, princesses, now it's time for math. Alyssa, Faellyn, and Vesta, go to Ms.Trixie. Willa, Octavia, and Kari go to Mrs.Hilde. Gwen, Yellia, and Rebbecca go to Mr. Adam. Chya and Bethany, stay with me. Now, I will leave a sign on the door in case you forget who your math teacher is." The princesses left the classroom except for Chya and Bethany who stayed for math.

After math, all the princesses went to gym class. "Hello," says Mr. Quinton. "We will do something fun for our gym class." Mr.Quinton pushed a button. A huge jungle gym appeared! And Willa's favorite band, Catchy Butterflies of Maryland came on the radio and it was her favorite song "We sing!" The princesses jumped. They climbed. They swung. Willa also jumped, climbed, and swung. It was about the best thing of Willa's life!

The princesses returned to class for social studies time. "Welcome back, class," Ms. Mikala said. "We will learn about rural, suburban, and urban communities." Yellia raised her hand.

"Yes, Yellia?" Ms. Mikala asked.

"Is there going to be a video?" Yellia asked.

"No." She pulled up an image. It was an apartment, a suburb home, and a barn. "The apartment is an example of an urban place. The house is a suburban place. The barn is a rural place. Now you must do a craft. You will have three options. Yes, Willa?" Ms. Mikala said.

"Is the craft that we create an urban, suburban, or rural diorama?" Willa asked.

"Yep," Ms. Mikala said. "Here's your cardboard and the three choices kit."

Ms. Mikala gave a kit to every princess. Willa was thinking: *Hmm. I'll do the rural one.* So Willa got the rural kit, and for a final touch, she added a well. The diorama was beautiful!

"RING," rang the bell. "Is it time to leave ALREADY?" Willa asked.

"Yep." said Lindsay.
She was on her way out from her class. So was Pia, Cecilia, and Hazel, along with other princesses.

"Bye, Willa," said Vesta, she is an art princess - the princess of volume.

"Bye, Vesta," Willa said.
Willa quickly remembered her bus number - 483! All the Water princesses climbed aboard. The bus flew and flew and flew.

"How was your day at school?" asked Cecilia.

"Great. I met all sorts of new kids- I mean, princesses," answered Willa. Cecilia smiled.
The bus whooshed down to the ground. "Whoa!" cried Willa as the bus landed.

"Bye." the bus driver said to Willa.

"See you tomorrow," Willa replied. The princesses walked to

their homes.

"I like the school, don't you?" asked Gwen.

"Yeah!!" Willa shouted. "I can't wait for tomorrow."

CHAPTER 3

What a ball!

On Friday, Willa was walking to her house from the bus stop. And other princesses came to her house too! All the Water princesses: Lindsay, Rebecca, Pia, Octavia, Cecilia, Gwen, Hazel, and Bethany, were right by her side walking to their homes.

"Ahh," Octavia sighed. "Fresh home air."

Gwen went to her gulf and thought about what to do that week. Gwen gasped, she had an idea! She touched her necklace to call the other Water princesses, and it glowed. The other Water Princesses' necklaces glowed too! "Water Princesses, I have an idea. I am bored, so why don't we make a warm treat stand?" called Gwen.

"That's a great idea! You know, guests are coming to stay with us all week, starting on Sunday!" said Bethany.

"Wait, **all** week? Okay, we can do a warm treats stand. I am looking forward to it!" called Pia. "Great, meet me at my gulf," Gwen said. So all the princesses went to Gwen's gulf.

"I've already got ideas," said Hazel. "We can make hot chocolate, and have pancakes, and have soup!"

"Yeah," Willa said.

"Who wants a snack?" Willa's dad asked, "I've been looking for all of you!"

"We wanna do a warm treats stand," Octavia explained. Willa's dad held nine soft pretzels and nine warm glasses of water.

"Hey, soft pretzels are warm, so why not do soft pretzels too?" said Willa. All the princesses agreed. Cecilia added water to the list too.

The next day Willa yawned as she woke up. The first thing she thought of was the warm treats stand. She burst up from her bed and got dressed. She rushed to her kitchen and grabbed some pancakes and warm muffins and ran to Gwen's gulf.

They ate pancakes, and Willa was ready for the long day ahead. She had written down:

> *Things for the Warm treats stand:*
> *1. Hot chocolate.*
> *2. Pancakes.*
> *3. Soup.*
> *4. Soft pretzels.*
> *5. Muffins.*
> *6. S'mores.*
> *7. Water from the well.*

"Willa?" asked Lindsay.

"Yeah?" said Willa.

"What are you writing?"

"Ideas for the warm treats stand," said Willa. It was Saturday; they had no time to lose!

"Hello?" called the mailman.

"Hi," called Octavia.

"Have you got some mail?" asked Bethany. The mailman held a brown package and one letter. "Thanks," called Willa's dad. "I ordered this package because it has decorations for the guests, and the letter is from me to all of you!"

Eagerly, Cecilia opened the package and found lots of decorations. All morning the princesses hung the things, but nobody was more excited than Willa.

"Let's do this hanger thingy before it's time for lunch!" said Willa. "Streamers, check. Balloons, check. Cake? Not checked."

"Here's the cake that I will put in the freezer," said Pia.

"Then cake, check!" said Willa.

"Looks like everything is ready for the warm treats stand... except for the warm treats," said Bethany.

"We can do that tomorrow," said Willa's mom and dad.

Early the next morning, at 5:00 am, Willa's doorbell rang.

"What is someone doing up at night?" she said as she stretched up from her bed. In her bathrobe, she spied downstairs to take a peek. She saw her parents at the door, and they were talking to someone Willa did not know.

"We would like to see princess Willa, please," said a man that was looking fancy. Willa knew she had to go up from her spot on the stairs and go back to her room. She pretended that she was asleep. So her parents came up and checked on her to tell that the special guests were here. They arrived from River Forest, an amazing town far away from Willa's home!

"Willa?" her mom called.

"Yes, Mom?" she said sleepily.

"The special guests are here. They would like to see you."
"Coming," Willa said. She got dressed in her dress as quickly as possible.

"Hello, Willa. I am Berk."

"Hi, Berk. How did you get here so early in the morning?" asked Willa.

"It took me 2 whole days to get here. I departed when it was Friday. But the problem was that it was so early, so it's early now, too!" answered Berk.

"Well, maybe we could set up the -" Willa's mom said, but just in the nick of time, Willa whispered, "It's a surprise."

Finally, at 8:00 a.m, the princesses call "Welcome to the warm treats stand!"

Berk was shocked, so was his wife, Elenora. "This is amazing!" shouted Elenora.

"Pancakes?" asked Willa.

"Of course," said Berk.

"Muffins?" asked Bethany.

"Yes, please," said Elenora. Together, they had a big breakfast!

"Mmm." said Rebbecca, "this is so good!"

"However did you make this food?" asked Berk and Elenora.

"Magic!" the princesses shouted at once.

"Now, what shall we do? I mean, I was looking forward to having a ball Saturday night," said Berk.

"Oh, the ball..." whispered Willa quietly. She smiled, "We'll have a surprise on Saturday night. In the meantime, why not look at these magazines?"

"Amazing! Who made these?" Elenora said.

"We did," said Octavia, she was a little bit nervous. Berk and Elenora smiled, the magazines looked kind of like the ones they have at the store.

◆ ◆ ◆

The following Saturday Berk announced, "Today is the day of the ball," Willa was terrified, she worried that her ball was not perfect, but on the other hand, she was excited!

"Where's the ball?" asked Elenora. Willa ran to the button that she wanted to push for the ball. "Here..." Pia said quietly.

BOOM!

There was a big party standing right in front of everyone!

"Oh, wow!" shouted Berk. All the people at the ball were dancing their night away.

"After the ball, let's have some s' mores, what do you think?"

asked the parents.

"YES!" everyone shouted.

"Hey, where's Bethany?" asked Willa.

Bethany was getting chocolate bars, graham crackers, and marsh-mallows. "S' mores!" said Bethany.

"These were made by the Water Princesses." Berk and Elenora said together.

CHAPTER 4

The new princess

Willa woke up one Saturday morning and was waiting by the mailbox, and Willa was super excited for the mail to come. Her mom told her that she would get something special in the mail. Soon there the mailman arrived! "Delivery for Willa," he said.

She eagerly opened it. It said:

Dear Willa and her family,
There is going to be a new Water Princess. Her name is Sylvie, and she has a cat named Auburn. Please get ready for her. Oh, she will be arriv-

ing at 10:00. Enjoy your day!
Love,
Sylvie's parents

Willa called the other Water princesses on her necklace. All of the girls and their families were excited, except for Bethany's parents. Bethany's dad was allergic to Munchkin cats, and Auburn was a Munchkin cat. Bethany's mom was allergic to Bombay cats and Russian blue cats, but she didn't know if she was allergic to Munchkin ones. Bethany was allergic to dogs - all kinds.

Pia's dad made a crown and a dress for Sylvie. Her mom was preparing and cleaning the floors. "I'm so confused. Why is there another princess?" asked Cecilia. Nobody knew. They prepared as hard as they could.

Suddenly, Sylvie arrived and exclaimed, "Lindsay, Rebecca, Pia, Octavia, Cecilia, Gwen, Hazel, Bethany, and Willa. What?"
The Water Princesses said together, "Please behold our new Water Princess: Sylvie, the princess of snow."

Bethany put Sylvie's crown on her head.

"Achoo!" Bethany's dad sneezed. He had to take his medicine to be safe. Luckily, Auburn was going to stay away from Bethany's parents. Sylvie was super excited that SHE became a Water princess! Her home was in a huge snowflake.

"Care for some water from the well?" Willa's mom asked.
"That would be great!" Sylvie replied. Willa decided to take her to her home in the snowflake. Sylvie loved it!

The next day was Sylvie's first day at Princess Elementary. She was disappointed not to be in Willa's class but was excited to be with Lindsay, Pia, Octavia, and Cecilia's class.

After a morning of LA, recess, lunch, and math, it was time for Sylvie's favorite: ART!

"Good afternoon, artists!" Ms. Alzena, their art teacher said.
"We are going to make a collage." There were newspapers, scraps, cardboard, old pom-poms, water bottles- almost anything! The princesses got to work and made beautiful crafts. Social studies was canceled because it was an early dismissal. Sylvie was happy because she was part of the crew!

"You are the best, Sylvie!" Willa exclaimed. Sylvie leaped around the Water Princesses and gave them a big hug. Then Sylvie made a thank-you card that said:

Dear Lindsay, Rebbecca, Pia, Octavia, Cecilia, Gwen, Hazel, Bethany, and Willa,

Thanks for lending me a hand in learning what it's like to be a Water Princess. I had fun at Princess Elementary and you can have fun with Auburn, too! I will hold a thank-you party tonight for being my sister friends! I hope you have a good day.

From,

Sylvie.

That night, the Water princesses had a thanks party in their neighborhood. There were glow sticks and lemonade and cupcakes and dancing!

After the party, the princesses decided to camp outside their houses! As they were getting into their sleeping bags, Sylvie said "Good night!"

"Good night," the Water princesses said back.

The Water princesses lived magically ever after.

POP QUIZZES!

Q1: Who places Willa's crown on her head?

1: Rebbecca
2: Hazel
3: Willa

Q2: What replaces this sentence: *Willa was very happy. She could not wait!*

1: *Willa was excited. She was jumping!*
2: *Willa was super nervous. She did not want to leave.*

Q3: Which schedule is correct?

1: Arrive,morning work,LA, recess, lunch,math,related arts,content,leave.
2: Leave,content,related arts,math,lunch,recess,LA,morning work, arrive.

Q4: Who is Willa's math teacher?

1: Mr.Adam
2: Mrs.Hilde
3. Mrs.Trixie

Q5: What are the names of the 2 fancy people that came to Willa's home?

A. Hilda/kjf and Hkjohfhjd;
B. Elenora and Berk
C. Sheena and Bradley

Q6: Did Sylvie have a cat?

    A.   No
    B.   Yes, and the cat's name is Mia.
    C.   Yes, and the cat's name is Auburn.

Answers:

Q1: Hazel places Willa's crown on her head.
Q2: *Willa was excited. She was jumping!*
Q3: Number 1 is the correct schedule.
Q4: Mrs.Hilde is Willa's math teacher.
Q5: Elenora and Berk are the 2 fancy people that came to Willa's home.
Q6: C is the correct answer, the cat's name is Auburn.

AFTERWORD

The proceeds for this book will go to The Water Project which supports communities in Africa by building access to clean, drinkable water. Learn more about this awesome organization at http://thewaterproject.com

You can contribute directly to Julia's campaign to raise money for a well in Africa by going to:

https://thewaterproject.org/community/profile/julias-waterproject

Made in the USA
Middletown, DE
06 December 2020

26458090R00018